The Twelve Dancing Princesses

The Twelve Dancing Princesses

Illustrated by ADRIENNE ADAMS

HOLT, RINEHART AND WINSTON   *New York   Chicago   San Francisco*

A Holt Owlet Book

Holt Owlet Books is a paperback picture book series, carefully chosen for merit and popularity from a distinguished backlist of children's literature.

Owlet Titles You May Enjoy:

Alexander, Lloyd
COLL AND HIS WHITE PIG
THE TRUTHFUL HARP

Belting, Natalia
THE SUN IS A GOLDEN EARRING

Caudill, Rebecca
A CERTAIN SMALL SHEPHERD
DID YOU CARRY THE FLAG
TODAY, CHARLEY?
A POCKETFUL OF CRICKET
THE BEST-LOVED DOLL
COME ALONG!

Cole, William
WHAT'S GOOD FOR A FOUR-YEAR-OLD?
WHAT'S GOOD FOR A FIVE-YEAR-OLD?
WHAT'S GOOD FOR A SIX-YEAR-OLD?

Jacobs, Leland
ALPHABET OF GIRLS
IS SOMEWHERE ALWAYS FAR AWAY?

Johnson, Crockett
WE WONDER WHAT WILL WALTER BE?
WHEN HE GROWS UP

Ness, Evaline
SAM,BANGS AND MOONSHINE
MR. MIACCA

NicLeodhas, Sorche
ALWAYS ROOM FOR ONE MORE
ALL IN THE MORNING EARLY

Stockton, Frank
THE BEE-MAN OF ORN
THE GRIFFIN AND THE MINOR CANNON

Wahl, Jan
CABBAGE MOON
COBWEB CASTLE

Wondriska, William
JOHN JOHN TWILLIGER
MR. BROWN AND MR. GRAY

Illustrations Copyright © 1966 by Adrienne Adams • All rights reserved, including the right to reproduce this book or portions thereof in any form Published simultaneously in Canada by Holt, Rinehart and Winston of Canada, Limited • Library of Congress Catalog Card Number: AC 66–10104

ISBN: 0-03-088502-7 • Printed in the United States of America

1 2 3 4 5 6 7 77 76 75 74 73 72

For
Elizabeth
Francis

Once upon a time there lived in the village of Montignies-sur-Roc a young cow-boy without father or mother. His real name was Michael, but he was always called the Star Gazer because when he drove his cows over the commons to seek for pasture, he went along with his head in the air, gaping at nothing.

The village girls used to cry after him, "Well, Star Gazer, what are you doing?" and Michael would answer, "Oh, nothing," and go on his way without even turning to look at them.

The fact was he thought them very ugly, with their sunburned necks, their great red hands, their coarse petti-

coats, and their wooden shoes. He had heard that some-where in the world there were girls who were always dressed in the finest silks and laces, and were called princesses. While his companions around the fire saw nothing in the flames but common everyday fancies, he dreamed that he had the happiness to marry a princess.

One morning about the middle of August, just at midday when the sun was hottest, Michael ate his dinner of a piece of dry bread, then he went to sleep under an oak. And while he slept he dreamt that there appeared before him a beautiful lady, dressed in a robe of cloth of gold, who said to him: "Go to the castle of Beloeil and there you shall marry a princess."

That evening the young cow-boy, who had been thinking a great deal about the advice of the lady in the golden dress, told his dream to the farm people. But, as was natural, they only laughed at the Star Gazer.

The next day at the same hour he went to sleep again under the same tree. The lady appeared before him a second time and said: "Go to the castle of Beloeil and you shall marry a princess."

In the evening Michael told his friends that he had dreamed the same dream again, but they only laughed at him more than before. "Never mind," he thought to himself, "if the lady appears to me a third time, I will do as she tells me."

The following day, to the great astonishment of all the village, about two o'clock in the afternoon a voice was heard singing:

> "Raleo, raleo,
> How the cattle go!"

It was the young cow-boy driving his herd back to the byre.

The farmer began to scold him furiously, but he answered quietly, "I am going away." He made his clothes into a bundle, said good-bye to all his friends, and boldly set out to seek his fortunes.

There was great excitement through all the village, and on the top of the hill the people stood holding their sides from laughter, as they watched the Star Gazer trudging bravely along the valley with his bundle at the end of his stick.

It was enough to make anyone laugh, certainly.

It was well known for full twenty miles round that there lived in the castle of Beloeil twelve princesses of wonderful beauty, as proud as they were beautiful, and who were so very sensitive and of such truly royal blood that they would have felt at once the presence of a pea in their beds even if the mattresses had been laid over it.

It was whispered about that they led exactly the lives that princesses ought to lead—sleeping far into the morning and never getting up till mid-day. They had twelve beds all in the same room, but what was very extraordinary was that although they were locked in by triple bolts every evening, every morning their satin shoes were found worn into holes.

When they were asked what they had been doing all night, they always answered that they had been asleep; and indeed, no noise was ever heard in the room, yet the shoes could not wear themselves out alone!

At last the Duke of Beloeil ordered the trumpet to be sounded and a proclamation to be made that whoever could discover how his daughters wore out their shoes could choose one of them for his wife.

On hearing the proclamation a number of princes arrived at the castle to try their luck. They watched all night behind the open door of the princesses, but when the morning came all the princes had disappeared, and no one could tell what had become of them.

When he reached the castle, Michael went straight to the gardener and offered his services. Now it happened that the garden boy had just been sent away, and though the Star Gazer did not not look very sturdy, the gardener agreed to take him as he thought that his handsome face would please the princesses.

Then Michael was told that when the princesses got up he was to present each one with a bouquet. Michael thought that if he had nothing more unpleasant to do than that he should get on very well.

Accordingly he placed himself behind the door of the princesses' room with the twelve bouquets in a basket. He gave one to each of the sisters, and they took them without even deigning to look at the lad, except Lina, the youngest, who fixed her large black eyes as soft as velvet on him and exclaimed, "Oh, how pretty he is—our new flower boy!" The rest all burst out laughing, and the eldest pointed out that a princess ought never to lower herself by looking at a garden boy.

Now Michael knew quite well what had happened to all the princes, but notwithstanding, the beautiful eyes of the Princess Lina inspired him with a violent longing to try his fate. Unhappily he did not dare to come forward, being

afraid that he would only be jeered at, or even turned away
from the castle on account of his impudence.

Nevertheless, the Star Gazer had another dream. The
lady in the golden dress appeared before him once more,

holding in one hand two young laurel trees—a cherry laurel and a rose laurel, and in the other hand a little golden rake, a little golden bucket, and a silken towel. She thus addressed him:

"Plant these two laurels in two large pots, rake them over with the rake, water them with the bucket, and wipe them with the towel. When they have grown as tall as a girl of fifteen, say to each of them, 'My beautiful laurel, with the golden rake I have raked you, with the golden bucket I have watered you, with the silken towel I have wiped you.' Then after that ask anything you choose and the laurels will give it to you."

Michael thanked the lady in the golden dress, and when he woke he found the two laurel bushes beside him. So he carefully obeyed the orders he had been given by the lady.

The trees grew very fast, and when they were as tall as a girl of fifteen he said to the cherry laurel, "My lovely cherry laurel, with the golden rake I have raked thee, with the golden bucket I have watered thee, with the silken towel I have wiped thee. Teach me how to become invisible." Then there instantly appeared on the laurel a pretty white flower which Michael gathered and stuck into his buttonhole.

That evening, when the princesses went upstairs to bed,
he followed them barefoot so that he might make no noise
and hid himself under one of the twelve beds so as not to
take up much room.

The princesses began at once to open their wardrobes and boxes. They took out the most magnificent dresses which they put on before their mirrors, and when they had finished, turned all around to admire their appearances.

Michael could see nothing from his hiding-place, but he could hear everything, and he listened to the princesses laughing and jumping with pleasure. At last the eldest said, "Be quick, my sisters, our partners will be impatient." At the end of an hour when the Star Gazer heard no more noise, he peeped out and saw the twelve sisters in splendid garments with their satin shoes on their feet, and in their hands the bouquets he had brought them.

"Are you ready?" asked the eldest.

"Yes," replied the other eleven in chorus and they took their places one by one behind her.

Then the eldest Princess clapped her hands three times and a trapdoor opened. All the princesses disappeared down a secret staircase and Michael hastily followed them.

As he was following in the footsteps of the Princess Lina, he carelessly trod on her dress.

"There is somebody behind me," cried the Princess; "someone is holding my dress."

"You foolish thing," said her eldest sister, "you are always afraid of something. It is only a nail which caught you."

They went down, down, down, till at last they came to

a passage with a door at one end which was only fastened with a latch. The eldest Princess opened it, and they found themselves immediately in a lovely little wood, where the leaves were spangled with drops of silver which shone in the brilliant light of the moon.

They next crossed another wood where the leaves were

sprinkled with gold, and after that still another, where the
leaves glittered with diamonds.

At last the Star Gazer perceived a large lake, and on the
shores of the lake twelve little boats with awnings, in which
were seated twelve princes who, grasping their oars,
awaited the princesses.

Each princess entered one of the boats, and Michael slipped into that which held the youngest princess. The boats glided along rapidly, but Lina's boat being heavier was always behind the rest. "We never went so slowly before," said the Princess. "What can be the reason?"

"I don't know," answered the Prince. "I assure you I am rowing as hard as I can."

On the other side of the lake the garden boy saw a beautiful castle splendidly illuminated, whence came the lively music of fiddles, kettledrums, and trumpets.

In a moment they touched land, and the company jumped out of the boats; and the princes, after securely fastening their barques, gave their arms to the princesses and conducted them to the castle.

Michael followed and entered the ballroom in their train. Everywhere were mirrors, lights, flowers, and damask hangings.

The Star Gazer was quite bewildered at the magnificence of the sight.

He placed himself out of the way in a corner, admiring the grace and beauty of the princesses. Their loveliness was of every kind. Some were fair and some were dark; some had chestnut hair, or curls still darker, and some had

golden locks. Never were so many beautiful princesses seen together at one time, but the one whom the cow-boy thought the most beautiful and the most fascinating was the little Princess with the velvet eyes.

With such eagerness she danced! Leaning on her partner's shoulder she swept by like a whirlwind. Her cheeks

flushed, her eyes sparkled, and it was plain that she loved dancing better than anything else.

The poor boy envied those handsome young men with whom she danced so gracefully, but he did not know how little reason he had to be jealous of them.

The young men were really the princes who, to the number of fifty at least, had tried to steal the princesses' secret. The princesses had made them drink of a philter

which froze the heart and left nothing but the love of dancing.

They danced until the shoes of the princesses were worn into holes. When the cock crowed the third time the fiddles stopped and a delicious supper was served, consisting of sugared orange flowers, crystallized rose leaves, powdered violets, cracknels, wafers, and other dishes, which are, as everyone knows, the favorite food of princesses.

After supper the dancers all went back to their boats, and this time the Star Gazer entered that of the eldest Princess. They crossed again the wood with the diamond-spangled leaves, the wood with gold-sprinkled leaves, and the wood whose leaves glittered with drops of silver, and as a proof of what he had seen, the boy broke a small branch from a tree in the last wood. Lina turned as she heard the noise made by the breaking of the branch.

"What was that noise?" she said.

"It was nothing," replied her eldest sister. "It was only the screech of the barn-owl that roosts in one of the turrets of the castle."

While she was speaking Michael slipped in front, ran up the staircase, and reached the princesses' room first. He flung open the window, slid down the vine which climbed up the wall, and found himself in the garden just as the sun was beginning to rise and it was time for him to set to his work.

That day when he made up the bouquets, Michael hid the branch with the silver drops in the nosegay intended for the youngest Princess.

When Lina discovered it she was much surprised. However, she said nothing to her sisters, but when she met the garden boy by accident while she was walking under the shade of the elms, she suddenly stopped as if to speak to him; then altering her mind, went on her way.

The same evening the twelve sisters went again to the ball, and the Star Gazer again followed them and crossed the lake in Lina's boat. This time it was the Prince who complained that the boat seemed very heavy.

"It is the heat," replied the Princess. "I, too, have been feeling very warm."

During the ball she looked everywhere for the garden boy, but she never saw him.

As they came back, Michael gathered a branch from the wood with the gold-spangled leaves, and now it was the eldest Princess who heard the noise that it made in breaking.

"It is nothing," said Lina, "only the cry of the barn-owl which roosts in the turrets of the castle."

As soon as she got up she found the branch in her bou-

quet. When the sisters went down she stayed a little behind and said to the garden-boy: "Where does this branch
come from?"

"Your Royal Highness knows well enough," answered Michael.

"So you have followed us?"

"Yes, Princess."

"How did you manage it? We never saw you."

"I hid myself," replied the Star Gazer quietly.

The Princess was silent a moment and then said:

"You know our secret! Keep it. Here is the reward for your discretion." And she flung the boy a purse of gold.

"I do not sell my silence," answered Michael and he went away without picking up the purse.

For three nights Lina neither saw nor heard anything extraordinary; on the fourth she heard a rustling among the diamond-spangled leaves of the wood. That day there was a branch from the trees in her bouquet.

She took the Star Gazer aside and said to him in a harsh voice: "You know what price my father has promised to pay for our secret?"

"I know, Princess," answered Michael.

"Don't you mean to tell him?"

"That is not my intention."

"Are you afraid?"

"No, Princess."
"What makes you so discreet, then?"
But Michael was silent.

Lina's sisters had seen her talking to the garden boy and jeered at her for it.

"What prevents your marrying him?" asked the eldest. "You would become a gardener too; it is a charming profession. You could live in a cottage at the end of the park and help your husband to draw up water from the well, and when we get up you could bring us our bouquets."

The Princess Lina was very angry, and when the Star Gazer presented her bouquet, she received it in a disdainful manner.

Michael behaved most respectfully. He never raised his eyes to her, but nearly all day she felt him at her side without ever seeing him.

One day she made up her mind to tell everything to her eldest sister.

"What!" said she, "this rogue knows our secret, and you never told me! I must lose no time in getting rid of him."

"But how?"

"Why, by having him taken to the tower with the dungeons, of course."

For this was the way that in old times beautiful princesses got rid of people who knew too much.

But the astonishing part was the youngest sister did not seem at all to relish this method of stopping the mouth of the garden boy who, after all, had said nothing to their father.

It was agreed that the question should be submitted to

the other ten sisters. All were on the side of the eldest.
Then the youngest sister declared that if they laid a finger
on the garden boy, she would go and tell their father the
secret of the holes in their shoes.

At last it was decided that Michael should be put to the
test; they would take him to the ball, and at the end of
supper would give him the philter which was to enchant
him like the other suitors.

They sent for the Star Gazer and asked him how he

had contrived to learn their secret; but still he remained silent.

Then, in commanding tones, the eldest sister gave him the order they had agreed upon.

He only answered, "I will obey."

He had really been present, invisible, at the council of princesses, and had heard all; but he had made up his mind to drink of the philter, and sacrifice himself to the happiness of the princess he loved.

Not wishing, however, to cut a poor figure at the ball by the side of the other dancers, he went at once to the laurels and said: "My lovely rose laurel, with the golden rake I have raked thee, with the golden bucket I have watered thee, with a silken towel I have dried thee. Dress me like a prince."

A beautiful pink flower appeared. Michael gathered it and found himself in a moment clothed in velvet which was as black as the eyes of the little Princess, with a cap to match, a diamond aigrette, and a blossom of rose laurel in his buttonhole.

Thus dressed, he presented himself that evening before the Duke of Beloeil and obtained leave to try and discover his daughters' secret. He looked so distinguished that hardly anyone would have known who he was.

The twelve princesses went upstairs to bed. Michael followed them and waited behind the open door till they gave the signal for departure.

This time he did not cross in Lina's boat. He gave his arm to the eldest sister, danced with each in turn, and was so graceful that everyone was delighted with him. At last

the time came for him to dance with the little Princess.
She found him the best partner in the world, but he did
not dare to speak a single word to her.

When he was taking her back to her place she said to
him in a mocking voice:

"Here you are at the summit of your wishes: you are
being treated like a prince."

"Don't be afraid," replied the Star Gazer gently. "You
shall never be a gardener's wife."

The little Princess stared at him with a frightened face,

and he left her without waiting for an answer.

When the satin slippers were worn through, the fiddles stopped, and the servants set the table. Michael was placed next to the eldest sister and opposite to the youngest.

They gave him the most exquisite dishes to eat and the most delicate wines to drink; and in order to turn his head more completely, compliments and flattery were heaped on him from every side.

But he took care not to be intoxicated, either by the wine or the compliments.

At last the eldest sister made a sign, and one of the pages brought in a large golden cup.

"The enchanted castle has no more secrets for you," she said to the Star Gazer. "Let us drink to your triumph."

He cast a lingering glance at the little Princess and without hesitation lifted the cup.

"Don't drink!" suddenly cried out the little Princess. "I would rather marry a gardener."

And she burst into tears.

Michael flung the contents of the cup behind him, sprang over the table, and fell at Lina's feet. The rest of the princes fell likewise at the knees of the princesses, each of whom chose a husband and raised him to her side. The charm was broken.

The twelve couples embarked in the boats, which crossed back many times to carry over the other princes. Then they all went through the three woods, and when they had passed the door of the underground passage a great noise was heard as if the enchanted castle was crumbling to the earth.

They went straight to the room of the Duke of Beloeil who had just awoke. Michael held in his hand the golden

cup, and he revealed the secret of the holes in the shoes.

"Choose, then," said the Duke, "whomever you prefer."

"My choice is already made," replied the garden boy
and he offered his hand to the youngest Princess who
blushed and lowered her eyes.

The Princess Lina did not become a gardener's wife; on the contrary, it was the Star Gazer who became a Prince; but before the marriage ceremony the Princess insisted that her lover tell her how he came to discover the secret.

So he showed her the two laurels which had helped him, and she, like a prudent girl, thinking they gave him too much advantage over his wife, cut them off at the root and threw them in the fire.

And this is why the country girls go about singing:

"Nous n'irons plus au bois,
Les lauriers sont coupés,"

and dancing in summer by the light of the moon.

About the Artist

One of the most distinguished and respected names in the field of children's book illustration, **Adrienne Adams** has twice been runner-up for the Caldecott Award. Her sensitive interpretations of three of the classic fairy tales have gained recognition as ALA Notable Books, and the rich variety and wide range of creativity for which her work is known, seen in her illustrations for CABBAGE MOON by Jan Wahl, is fully expressed in her elegant pictures for Andrew Lang's THE TWELVE DANCING PRINCESSES.